First published in the United States by
Ideals Publishing Corporation
Nashville, Tennessee 37214

First published in Denmark by
Gyldendal, Copenhagen, Denmark

Printed in Portugal 1990

ISBN 0-8249-8488-9

Library of Congress Card Catalog Number 90-082449

# Wildebeest

By Franz Berliner
Illustrated by Lilian Brøgger

Ideals Children's Books • Nashville, Tennessee

From horizon to horizon, the vast Serengeti plain was filled with fleeing animals.

In the mountains N'gai, who was the animals' god, rumbled and grumbled.

That was why the animals fled. They were afraid of N'gai. In headlong flight, they thundered over the wide plain: hundreds of elephants, hundreds and hundreds of giraffes, thousands of buffalo, thousands and thousands of zebra, antelope, gazelle, and warthogs.

And one wildebeest.

As they pounded and pounded along, the whole world shook.

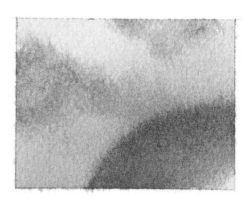

Suddenly, they stopped and stood to listen. N'gai stopped his rumbling and grumbling, and they knew that he was about to say something, because he usually spoke in the calm after the storm.

He spoke and his voice was severe and booming.

"Wild Beast!" he roared. "You are making too much noise. You are pounding too hard. Much too hard, Wild Beast!"

The wildebeest bowed his head humbly. More than that, he knelt on his forelegs and laid his head on the ground.

The black clouds disappeared. The sun came out, and once again the world became the place it should be.

The other animals shook their heads and said to the wildebeest, "Why do you always have to be so wild?"

Wild Beast became furious. He charged, lowering his head with its sharp horns and then leaping at the other animals.

But in mid-leap, he hesitated and threw his head to one side, trying to turn away. He was not so brave as he wanted to believe.

But his body wouldn't turn—it continued forward at full speed. He stumbled and he kept from falling by kicking up sideways. Unfortunately, he made himself look very silly.

The wildebeest turned away from the others in embarrassment. He hung his head low as his scraggly beard waved gloomily under his chin.

Why do I always have to be so wild? he asked himself.

That's an easy one, he answered. Just look at me! A head like a horse, horns like a cow, beard like a goat, mane like a lion, trunk like a giraffe, legs like a deer, and a tail like a donkey. N'gai must have made me from spare parts left over from his creation work.

What do I have that is all my own? Only my wildness! What would I be without that?

Nothing! If I keep my wildness, at least I will be something.

13

So Wild Beast continued to be wild.

He didn't want to be with the others. When the others came near, he snorted, shook his head, jumped up and down, and shouted, "Mind your own business! Leave me alone!"

But deep inside he was so lonely. On the other hand, he didn't know how to change.

A wildebeest is a wildebeest is a wildebeest.

"Keep off! Stay away!" he would cry.

One day he found a small, hidden valley. Its narrow entrance was almost impossible to detect.

It was a beautiful little valley with acacia trees and scrub bushes. And best of all, the valley's lush grass sprouted and grew again just as fast he could eat it.

Oh, my favorite food, he thought.

The wildebeest thought, this shall be my valley, the most secret valley in the world. No one shall see it—no one shall get as much as one blade of grass, not even one little sprout!

And he guarded his secret so well that no one discovered it. If the others headed toward the little valley, he drove them away by making wild leaps and jumps. The others would stop and stand staring, shaking their heads, asking, "How can he be so wild?"

But, one day, something happened.

Great herds of animals came from the south into the vast plain. They were miserable and dirty, with haggard bodies and hanging heads. With glazed eyes and dusty skin, they came limping and staggering, nearly unable to drag themselves along.

Wild Beast stared at them in surprise. Among the ravaged herds, he recognized members of his own tribe!

"I thought I was the only wildebeest in the whole world," he said to them.

"Oh, no," the newcomers sighed and groaned. "We were once a great and proud nation in the south. But now only the sad remains are left.

"Most of our calves are already gone. Some starved to death and others were stolen by the big cats.

"Both the big rain and the small rain failed. If we can't find new, lush grass soon, not even the survivors will be left."

Wild Beast thought of his secret valley. Should I? he thought.

No! Why should I share? What is mine is mine! I am wild, wild, wild, and I will always stay wild.

But deep in his soul a thought whispered, "No. No one can be that wild. No one with a heart."

Ashamed, Wild Beast hurried to lead the tribe to the secret valley.

Strangely enough, sharing his valley made him so happy that he forgot all about his wildness.

He even showed the valley to a herd of long-legged, staggering gazelle. He shared it with zebra who were so skinny that no one could tell their stripes from their ribs.

The wildebeest's gladness grew, filling him totally and satisfying him more than the greenest green blades of grass.

Now, with the passing of his wildness, Wild Beast learned about being with the others.

When the herd left the secret valley, he followed it. He showed his new tribe to a safe crossing over the dangerous Mara river—and none of the new calves were lost.

He stayed with the herd. From that time on, all wildebeest have traveled with many others. They move with gazelle and antelope, they graze with zebra and other four-footed creatures, and they even roam with the two-legged ostriches.

When they pass the old rhinoceros, Kifaru, the wildebeest let him know it is they by coughing respectfully because Kifaru's small, near-sighted eyes can't see them very well. This tells him that they are not strange and dangerous creatures.

They carefully watch the giraffe because he can see danger when it's far away. And they listen to the advice of the old elephant because she has heard so much with her huge, fanning ears and has never forgotten a bit of it.

But they keep the lions and the packs of hyenas, jackals, and wild dogs at a distance.

N'gai, their god who could see and hear everything, saw the change in Wild Beast. One day, he spoke to him again. This time his voice was not so severe and booming, but more like a breeze in the trees along the river.

"Wild Beast," he said, "from now on, you shall no longer be called a wildebeest. I have found a name for you, which is soft and nice. From this day, you shall be called gnu."

And that was how the gnu got its name. And gnu it has been called ever since, in many languages around the world.

*Postscript*

Wildebeest is an English name for the gnu—originally coming from the language of the Boers. Gnu is an African name, from the language of the Bushmen.

If you say gnu slowly, you will hear how soft and nice it sounds.